Yoga Tales from the Gym

Everybody's GOOD at Something

Written by
Susan E. Rose

Illustrated by
Emily Hercock

CIP: Publisher's Cataloging-in-Publication data

Names: Rose, Susan E., Author. | Hercock, Emily J., Illustrator.
Title: Everybody's good at something : Yoga tales from the gym
/ written by Susan E Rose; illustrated by Emily J. Hercock.
Series: Yoga Tales from the Gym

Description: Tarpon Springs, FL: Susan Rose Yoga, 2021. | Summary: Katie learns self esteem
and confidence when Miss Bendy, PE and yoga teacher, introduces the class to yoga poses.

Identifiers: LCCN: 2021903840
ISBN: 978-1-7367132-1-1 (hardcover)
978-1-7367132-0-4 (paperback)
978-1-7367132-2-8 (ebook)

Subjects: LCSH Yoga—Juvenile fiction. | Self-esteem—Juvenile fiction. | School—Juvenile fiction.
| Physical education and training—Juvenile fiction. | CYAC Yoga—Fiction. | Self-esteem—
Fiction. | School—Fiction. | Physical education and training—Fiction. | BISAC JUVENILE
FICTION / Sports & Recreation / General | JUVENILE FICTION / Health & Daily Living / Daily
Activities | JUVENILE FICTION / Imagination & Play | JUVENILE FICTION / Social Themes /
Self-Esteem & Self-Reliance Classification: LCC PZ7.1 .R67 Eve 2021 | DDC [E]—dc23

Layout and Design by Louie Romares

For kids' yoga resources, visit:
@susanroseyoga
www.susanroseyoga.com
www.facebook.com/susanroseauthor

Dedication

This book is dedicated to all children like Katie, who sometimes struggle to discover what they do well. Keep looking, keep trying—until you find your own special gifts. Then share those gifts with the world.

Acknowledgements

A special thank you to all my former teachers for your influence and for helping me to become the teacher I am today. I can still hear your encouraging voices in my mind!

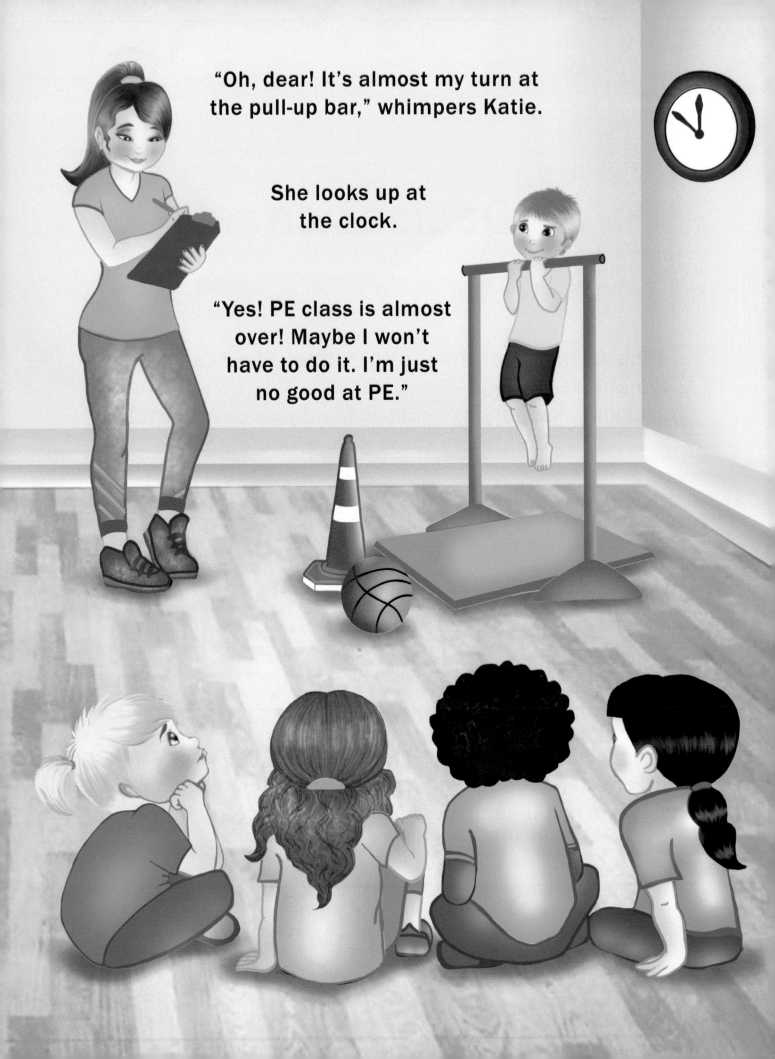

"Oh, dear! It's almost my turn at the pull-up bar," whimpers Katie.

She looks up at the clock.

"Yes! PE class is almost over! Maybe I won't have to do it. I'm just no good at PE."

Katie knows that her brother is really good at basketball

And her best friend is really good at soccer.

Katie wonders,

What am I good at?

Miss Bendy calls her name. "You're next, Katie."
Oh, no! It's my turn, thinks Katie. She hopes the bell
will ring before she gets to the pull-up bar.

She can hear the other kids laughing behind her back. "This should be funny!" one of the boys says.

Katie grips the bar with both hands. She tries to raise her feet, but... down she goes. "I'm just no good at the pull-up bar," she tells Miss Bendy.

The next week in PE, Miss Bendy says, "Let's all jump rope today. Just throw the rope over your head, then jump when it hits the ground."

Katie tries and tries to jump over the rope. But the more she tries, the more tangled she becomes. "I'm just no good at jump rope," she tells Miss Bendy.

A week later, Miss Bendy says, "Everyone find a ball and start dribbling around the gym!" Katie finds a basketball.

But she is not able to dribble it at all. The ball keeps bouncing away from her. "I'm just no good at dribbling," she cries.

Katie wonders,

Will I ever find something I AM good at?

But the following week in PE, things look different. There are no balls or jump ropes anywhere. The lights have been dimmed. There is soft music playing. Long blue mats are lined up on the floor.

Katie is confused.
She thinks,

What's THIS all about?

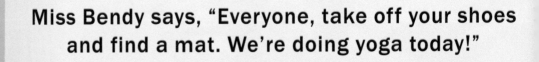

Miss Bendy says, "Everyone, take off your shoes and find a mat. We're doing yoga today!"

"What's yoga?" the children ask, looking befuddled.

"Let's find out!" is the answer.

Everyone follows Miss Bendy's lead and takes their shoes off. Then they each sit on a long blue yoga mat.

"Sit criss-cross, and rest your hands on your knees. This is called Easy Seat. Then take a deep breath in and blow it out slowly, like you are blowing out a candle. This sends a message to your body to slow down. Let's try it a few times. Inhale... and exhale... inhale...and exhale. Notice how that makes you feel. Do you feel calmer now?"

Hey, I DO feel a little better,

Katie notices.

"Now stretch your legs out long," says Miss Bendy,
"and wiggle your toes. Stretch your arms over
your head. Then reach out for your toes.
It's OK if you can't touch them. This is called Forward
Fold. It stretches the back of your body."

"Now come to your hands and knees," says Miss Bendy, "and make what's called Table Pose. Can you reach one leg back? Then reach the opposite arm forward? Hold steady!

This is called Spinal Balance.
It helps to strengthen your center.
Now let's do the other side!"
Katie is actually enjoying PE.

Gosh, I can hold Spinal
Balance for a long time.

Miss Bendy tells the class to come back to Table Pose. "Now tuck your toes under. Can you lift your hips up to the sky? Keep your arms straight and look at your feet. This is called Downward Facing Dog. It will make your arms strong and stretch your legs."

Katie thinks,

This is simple!

"Now come down onto your belly and take a rest. Turn your head and put your cheek on your hands. Can you feel your belly breathing against the floor? This is called Crocodile Pose.

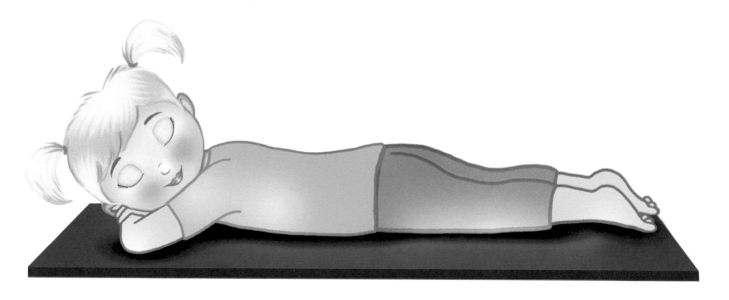

Now place your hands on the mat under your shoulders. Lift your head and straighten your arms. This is Snake Pose. Can you feel it stretching the front of your body?"

Katie lifts her head up high.

Oh, this feels so good!

"Let's push our hips back and sit on our heels. Now bring your head down to the mat. Rest here in Child's Pose for a few breaths."

This is kind of fun,

thinks Katie, as she breathes in and out.

"Now, everyone stand in the center of your mat. Stretch your arms down and out to the side. Lift your heart and look straight ahead. This is Mountain Pose. Stand so strong that nothing can topple you!"

Easy peasy,
thinks Katie,
I feel as strong as a mountain!

"Let's become warriors," says Miss Bendy. "Step one foot forward and bend your knee. Keep your back leg nice and straight. Reach your arms up and say, 'I am Strong!' This pose is Strong Warrior.

Then turn your belly to the side and reach your arms out wide. Say, 'I am Brave!' This is Brave Warrior.

Now reach one hand down and one hand up. Say, 'I can do anything!' This is Proud Warrior."

Katie feels strong.

I CAN do anything!

Some of her classmates are getting
a little confused—and tired of
holding the poses. But not Katie!
She can hold them all day long.

"Great job, Katie!" says Miss Bendy.
"You are a natural at yoga!"

The class could see how well
Katie held all the yoga poses.

Finally, they come to the last pose of the class. "This is called Tree Pose," says Miss Bendy. "Stand tall on one foot. Bring the other foot to the side of your leg. Stretch your arms over your head— just like the branches of a tree. How long can you balance?

If you fall, it's OK, just try again!"

Katie balances longer than anyone!

"Wow, Katie, you are really good at yoga!" one of the boys says.

Katie feels wonderful. Katie feels confident.

Her reason is simple:

"Well, everybody's good at SOMETHING!"

Notes to Parents and Teachers:

Yoga is an ancient art and science that has real-world benefits for children today. Yoga means to yoke, or bring together, the mind, body and spirit. Practicing yoga can help children increase their physical fitness, improve their mental focus, and boost their self-esteem and confidence.

When practicing yoga with children, keep in mind that yoga exercises should never cause discomfort. If something hurts, that is a message from the body saying, "don't stretch so far right now." Teaching children to listen to their bodies is an important part of the practice. Our bodies are really smart!

Breathing is an important part of yoga. We inhale through the nose to warm and filter the air, and exhale through either our nose or mouth. Yoga breathing takes a while to learn, so be patient with your child—and with yourself!

Yoga is about doing your best, but it is not about being perfect. That's why we call it a "yoga practice." Yoga teaches us concentration and body control. It also teaches us to keep trying, especially if a pose is hard to do at first.

It's important to have fun doing yoga! It is something you can enjoy throughout the rest of your life! Practicing yoga can lead to a lifetime of fun, fitness, and feeling great!

SPECIAL NOTE TO READERS:

If you enjoyed the book, please leave a review at bit.ly/Katiereview so others will be able to find it.

Share a picture of your child on Instagram, either holding or reading the book. Be sure to tag @susanroseyoga.

Sign up to receive free kids' yoga resources and updates on the series Yoga Tales from the Gym at www.susanroseyoga.com

Check out Susan's other book, Let's Make a Rainbow: a Yoga Story for Kids, available at www.susanroseyoga.com

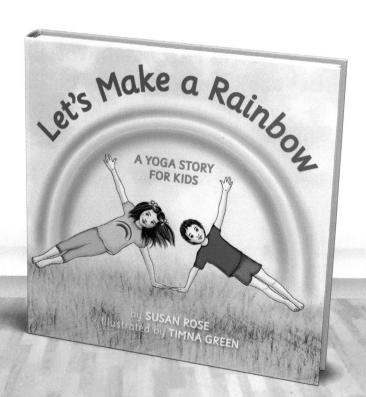

ABOUT THE AUTHOR:

Susan Rose is a Certified YOGAKIDS™ Teacher with a Masters Degree in Physical Education. She has taught gymnastics, fitness and yoga to children of all ages for many years. Susan loves helping children become more comfortable with their bodies through yoga. As they discover what they can do, children gain confidence and feel good about themselves.

Susan and her husband Fritz live in Tarpon Springs, Florida. Her first book, Let's Make a Rainbow: A Yoga Story for Kids, was published in December 2020 and is available on www.susanroseyoga.com.

ABOUT THE ILLUSTRATOR:

Emily Hercock has been drawing from the moment she could hold a pen! She has now been illustrating professionally for 6 years and has just started a Self Publishing Services business with her husband Michael who edits manuscripts and formats and designs book layout under the name Hercock Self Publishing Services. Emily and Michael live in a small country village in Norfolk, UK with their cat Dougal. "Drawing truly is my first love and I have now illustrated over 40 books many of which can be found on Amazon and in libraries and bookshops.

Made in the USA
Columbia, SC
05 August 2024

40014893R00022